My Brother's Blue

Gary Raines

Gary Raines

Illustrations by Joshua Allen

AuthorHouse™
1663 Liberty Drive
Bloomington, IN 47403
www.authorhouse.com
Phone: 1-800-839-8640

First published by AuthorHouse   11/9/2009

ISBN: 978-1-4490-4185-4 (sc)

Library of Congress Control Number: 2009911215

Printed in the United States of America
Bloomington, Indiana

This book is printed on acid-free paper.

authorHOUSE®

For my daughter,
who loves to read.

Blue was a black kitten, but we named her Blue because she had deep blue eyes. Mom said they were the type of eyes that could see into your soul. I believe she was right.

Blue never cared for people. We seemed to be nothing more than the things who fed her and changed her litter box. When she wasn't lurking under the sofa waiting to swat at our toes, she would stretch out on the carpet and stare at one of us with those deep blue eyes. All of that changed the day my baby brother was brought home from the hospital.

I was very excited the day he arrived; Blue was not. Another human in the house was nothing to be happy about. As soon as she had the chance, Blue crept up to my brother for a closer look. I watched as she glared at him, and I held my breath as she leaned in for a closer look, but Blue, who had never shown kindness to anyone, nuzzled up to my brother's face and began to purr. From that moment on, she rarely left his side.

When my mom changed his diapers, Blue was there. When he ate, Blue was there. When he napped, Blue usually napped with him. Her only time alone was spent in the field of wildflowers behind our house. I would watch as she vanished amid a rainbow of colored petals, returning only when my brother's voice was heard once again. Mom and Dad would say how lucky David was to have such a devoted friend. They didn't know yet how true those words were.

At first, David seemed like every other baby, but as he grew everyone realized there was something different about my brother. He never reacted to my mother's warm smile or smiled himself. When someone would try to pick him up, he would arch his back and cry out. He almost never looked another person in the eye or showed interest in other people. Blue was the only one he seemed to love.

As David grew older, his odd behavior became easier to see. He would pick a toy up and place it right back down for hours at a time or switch a light on and off over and over again. He would tilt his head when he looked at an object and topple over as he lost his balance. I must admit, I found his toppling very funny; my parents did not.

Mom and Dad began talking to doctors about things I was too young to understand. I knew they were worried David was going to hurt himself. I wasn't worried at all. After all, Blue was always there to protect him. A short time later, I wasn't as sure.

everyone was in bed when I first heard the thump. THUMP! Then there was silence. THUMP! More silence. Then THUMP! again. As I raced into my brother's room, the thump was replaced by a cat's cry. I switched on the light just in time to see Blue between my brother and the wooden board at the front of his bed. David was rocking back and forth; with each backward motion he fell into Blue. Just then, my mother came rushing past me. I watched as she picked up my brother. When she did, Blue slumped onto the mattress. She couldn't speak, but those deep blue eyes were pleading for help.

Selflessly, Blue had placed herself between my brother's head and the headboard. For her bravery, she received two broken ribs and the adoration of my parents. My brother received only a few bruises. His injuries could have been much worse.

After that night, people started coming to our house to observe David and ask my parents questions. Sometimes my parents would take him places and leave me with a baby sitter. When they did, Blue would pace the windowsills frantically until my brother returned.

Finally, after months of tests, questions and observations, the doctors felt they had an answer. My brother was autistic. I remember my mom telling me David was special because his mind worked differently, but I already knew he was special. Blue had taught me that.

As time went by, we learned to cope with my brother's autism. Everything in our house had its place and every activity had its special time of the day. Even David's bath water had to be the correct temperature. Through it all, Blue was watchful. If I overslept, and my brother was left alone, Blue was sure to wake me with a bite on the nose; when David's bath water was too warm, my mom would receive a disgusted glare.

My brother grew up as Blue grew old. He learned to speak better than most people with autism, but he usually talked at people and not to them. He usually needed help dressing himself in the morning, but he could make his own breakfast of cereal and orange juice without any trouble. Still, as months turned into years, Blue remained his only friend.

Blue was fifteen years old when she died. She had been sleeping on my brother's lap and never woke up. I will never forget the tears that streamed down his face as he spoke.

"Mom, Blue died," he said. "Bury her with flowers. She deserves flowers.

e buried Blue in the midst of her wildflowers. None of us spoke as my brother placed her into the ground; no one knew what to say. Mom worried about how David would cope with Blue's passing, but his days went on as they always had. Months later, the doctors said he may have forgotten Blue, but I knew they were mistaken.

I remember one day like it was yesterday. I had just rolled out of bed, and I knew David would be eating his cereal at the kitchen table. Curiously, as I entered the kitchen, he was nowhere to be found. For a moment I was frantic, but then, remembering the day, I dashed out the back door and into the field. There, next to Blue's grave, sat my brother. Blue had died exactly one year ago.

For 364 days a year his routine barely changes from one day to the next. But on this day, from sunup to sundown, he leaves our world to be with his friend. Sometimes we join him, but usually we leave him to his thoughts. After all, she was never truly our cat. She was always my brother's Blue.